Samuel French Acting Edition

Roz and Ray

by Karen Hartman

SAMUELFRENCH.COM   SAMUELFRENCH.CO.UK

Copyright © 2019 by Karen Hartman
All Rights Reserved

ROZ AND RAY is fully protected under the copyright laws of the United States of America, the British Commonwealth, including Canada, and all other countries of the Copyright Union. All rights, including professional and amateur stage productions, recitation, lecturing, public reading, motion picture, radio broadcasting, television and the rights of translation into foreign languages are strictly reserved.

ISBN 978-0-573-70751-3

www.SamuelFrench.com
www.SamuelFrench.co.uk

FOR PRODUCTION ENQUIRIES

UNITED STATES AND CANADA
Info@SamuelFrench.com
1-866-598-8449

UNITED KINGDOM AND EUROPE
Plays@SamuelFrench.co.uk
020-7255-4302

Each title is subject to availability from Samuel French, depending upon country of performance. Please be aware that *ROZ AND RAY* may not be licensed by Samuel French in your territory. Professional and amateur producers should contact the nearest Samuel French office or licensing partner to verify availability.

CAUTION: Professional and amateur producers are hereby warned that *ROZ AND RAY* is subject to a licensing fee. Publication of this play(s) does not imply availability for performance. Both amateurs and professionals considering a production are strongly advised to apply to Samuel French before starting rehearsals, advertising, or booking a theatre. A licensing fee must be paid whether the title(s) is presented for charity or gain and whether or not admission is charged. Professional/Stock licensing fees are quoted upon application to Samuel French.

No one shall make any changes in this title(s) for the purpose of production. No part of this book may be reproduced, stored in a retrieval system, or transmitted in any form, by any means, now known or yet to be invented, including mechanical, electronic, photocopying, recording, videotaping, or otherwise, without the prior written permission of the publisher. No one shall upload this title(s), or part of this title(s), to any social media websites.

For all enquiries regarding motion picture, television, and other media rights, please contact Samuel French.

MUSIC USE NOTE

Licensees are solely responsible for obtaining formal written permission from copyright owners to use copyrighted music in the performance of this play and are strongly cautioned to do so. If no such permission is obtained by the licensee, then the licensee must use only original music that the licensee owns and controls. Licensees are solely responsible and liable for all music clearances and shall indemnify the copyright owners of the play(s) and their licensing agent, Samuel French, against any costs, expenses, losses and liabilities arising from the use of music by licensees. Please contact the appropriate music licensing authority in your territory for the rights to any incidental music.

IMPORTANT BILLING AND CREDIT REQUIREMENTS

If you have obtained performance rights to this title, please refer to your licensing agreement for important billing and credit requirements.

ROZ AND RAY premiered at Seattle Repertory Theatre (Braden Abraham, Artistic Director; Jeffrey Herrmann, Managing Director) on October 14, 2016, running through November 13, 2016. The production was directed by Chay Yew, with set design by Tim Mackabee, costume design by Rose Pederson, lighting design by Geoff Korf, original music and sound design by Christopher Kriz, dramaturgy by Kristin Leahey, PhD, stage management by Erin B. Zatlotka, and assistant direction by Lia Fakhouri. The cast was as follows:

ROZ .... Ellen McLaughlin
RAY .... Teagle F. Bougere

ROZ AND RAY co-premiered at Victory Gardens Theater in Chicago, Illinois (Chay Yew, Artistic Director) on November 11, 2016, running through December 11, 2016. The production was directed by Chay Yew, with set design by Tim Mackabee, costume design by Christine Pascual, lighting design by Diane D. Fairchild, original music and sound design by Christopher Kriz, dramaturgy by Isaac Gomez, stage management by Amanda J. Davis, and assistant direction by Arianna Soloway. The cast was as follows:

ROZ .... Mary Beth Fisher
RAY .... James Vincent Meredith

ROZ AND RAY was commissioned and developed with support from the Playwrights' Center's McKnight Commission and Residency Program (Minneapolis, Minnesota) and was also supported by Hedgebrook, the Alley All New Festival, the Seattle Repertory Theatre Writers Group, and an Edgerton Foundation New Play Award.

CHARACTERS

ROZ – Fiftyish, playing as young as late thirties. Warm and direct. She usually wears a lab coat. Caucasian. From Ohio.

RAY – Fortyish, playing as young as late twenties. Capable of great love and great rage. Latino, African-American, or Caucasian. From Texas. If the actor playing Ray is Latino, Ray's last name is pronounced Lé*on*.

SETTING

Medical and home locations in San Diego, California.

TIME

1976 through 1987, and a single day in 1991.

AUTHOR'S NOTES

The dates and text in **bold** at the top of each scene should be indicated by projection, voice-over, or signs.

The scenes flow fluidly, in most cases without transitional music or sound. Therefore the actors will generally stay in the same clothes. Exceptions are indicated. Although Roz gets a promotion and a new office in 1987, we probably don't see a big change.

Phone calls are better without physical phones, in keeping with the fluid transitions. If it's hard to make clear that Roz's monologues at the top are phone calls, she can have a desktop phone.

It helps to remember that Ray's unseen sons Mikey and Ray Ray are at the center of Roz and Ray's lives. This ongoing mutual priority keeps the pleasure of their connection from getting too casual.

Overlapping text is indicated by a slash (/) where the next character's line begins.

Dialogue in parentheses is implied, not spoken.

In loving memory of Dr. Gary Hartman

1976

(San Diego Children's Hospital.)

*(**ROZ**, late thirties, sits on a doctor's stool, wearing a lab coat and a clown nose.)*

*(**RAY**, late twenties, sits next to her in a regular chair, wearing nicely kept working-class clothes.)*

(Her stool might be higher than his chair.)

*(They face Ray's twin sons, age seven, unseen. **ROZ** is warm, comfortable, and direct. **RAY** is out of his element.)*

ROZ. Here we go!

I'm going to show you how to inject a magic medicine.

I will use a needle, and soon you will be the needle experts, the needle twins; my goodness you boys will be the needle superheroes!

Look at you boys.

I am so happy to meet you today.

(One child cries. We don't hear him.)

Oh no.

RAY. *(Stern.)* Mikey don't you cry this is fun.

*(**ROZ** takes off the nose.)*

ROZ. No clowns. Just me.

Better already? Good for you.

(The other child laughs. We don't hear him.)

RAY. *(Stern again.)* Ray Ray don't you laugh this is serious.

ROZ. It is pretty silly.

(She plays with the clown nose, on and off.)

ROZ. Clown.

Doctor Roz.

Clown.

Doctor Roz.

Did you know that we can't learn when we're scared? It's true. So if I'm ever explaining something, and you get scared, you tell me, okay? I want you both to understand what's going on, so you can take good care of your bodies.

Ready to learn?

(She demonstrates.)

I clean my hands with antiseptic, and my skin.

I use a disposable needle.

I draw the Factor VIII – mine is saline but yours will be genuine Factor VIII!

I draw just past the blue line here, then push the syringe so I see a drop of fluid...

(To **RAY.***)* This is important. You don't want to waste medication, but you need to see that liquid. An air bubble will cause a real problem.

(Back to the boys.) I'll stick myself first, then you can stick Dad and me.

(Quick glance at **RAY.***)*

Or just me.

Then you can each stick yourselves!

I find the vein.

(Patting her arm at the crook of the elbow.) I have to pat pat pat pat pat pat pat.

Ah, there it is.

I pop the needle right into the vein.

I push the plunger.

Done.

It will take a little longer when you do this because you need to get all that good medicine.

Ready Mikey? Ready Ray Ray?

RAY. Do what the nice nurse says.
ROZ. I'm a doctor.
RAY. *(Mortified.)* Excuse me, ma'am.
ROZ. Please call me Doctor. Doctor Kagan, or Doctor Roz.
RAY. *(Again mortified.)* Pardon me. We never had a doctor take so much time. At Edgemoor we saw a nurse.
ROZ. Oh. Good. I am a different kind of doctor.
RAY. Do what the doctor says.
ROZ. Once they learn the procedure, they can inject the Factor three times a week. They don't need to wait for a bleed. They can self-inject at home.
RAY. What about transfusions?

> (**ROZ** *holds up a vial of medicine.*)

That's it?
ROZ. We're done with the Dark Ages. I came to help open a state-of-the-art hematology-oncology unit right here at San Diego Children's.
What do you boys like to do?
RAY. Sports.
ROZ. What's your favorite?
RAY. Ray Ray begs to do Pop Warner but I said no way.
ROZ. Your kids can play football.
RAY. Don't mess with their heads ma– Doctor.
ROZ. Life expectancy for a hemophiliac boy born today is seventy years.

> *(That's a miracle.)*

RAY. Seventy years. That's / normal.
ROZ. Normal.

> (**ROZ** *and* **RAY** *look at each other, then back at the boys.*)

Are you ready to inject Doctor Roz?

> *(They aren't ready.)*

RAY. Show respect.

ROZ. You're seven; you decide when you're ready.

Would you like to know a little more about the magic medicine first?

Okay. Do you ever bake cookies? With your / mom?

RAY. No.

ROZ. Well. You need all the ingredients. For cookies, for your body, for any project. Your blood is missing one ingredient, called clotting factor. So in the past, a hospital would pump you full of blood, and cryo, all those transfusions, right? But now:

>   *(Holds up vial of medicine.)*

An advanced laboratory spins hundreds of gallons of blood, bathtubs of blood, a swimming pool of blood, and they separate it with big motors to extract this –

>   *(The vial.)*

Factor VIII. All that blood, concentrated. To deliver your missing ingredient, so that when you get a cut or a bruise, your body can heal.

This is precious. For you.

>   *(Another bottle.)*

This is saline. For Doc Roz.

Who remembers how to fill the needle?

RAY. Careful, Ray Ray.

>   *(**ROZ** offers the syringe and vial to the boy.)*

ROZ. Go ahead. You won't hurt me.

1991

>   *(**RAY** rises straight from his chair. He's now in his early forties.)*
>
>   *(He holds up a sign: "Dr. Roz Kagan Killed My Son." **RAY** yells with all his might:)*

RAY. DOCTOR ROZ KAGAN KILLED MY SON.

DOCTOR ROZ KAGAN KILLED MY SON.
DOCTOR ROZ KAGAN KILLED MY SON.
DOCTOR ROZ KAGAN KILLED MY SON.
DOCTOR ROZ KAGAN KILLED MY SON.
DOCTOR ROZ KAGAN KILLED MY SON.
DOCTOR ROZ KAGAN KILLED MY SON!

(ROZ, in her office, now fiftyish. She lets the phone ring. Then:)

ROZ. This is Doctor Kagan.

Tom, my old friend. Gina's good? Kids are good? You still – what is it, windsurfing? Old dog new tricks, you old dog.

Yeah I hear him. It would be hard not to –

Sure I remember Ray Leon. I remember all my –

Will I make time to speak with you? When did we start saying that, "make time," did Reagan's people invent that? Even time is something you can just make if you've got the gumption? We'll never see the eighties again, and that's a silver lining.

Tom. Tom tom tom tom tom. You know me. You have seen me. Done feature after feature. I don't need to cover my ass at this point; I don't care about that. You know the physician I am.

You need a statement.

Sometimes you're the good guy, sometimes you're the bad guy, sometimes you're just a guy in a shitstorm.

That's my statement.

I like you Tom, I do, I hope life's going better in your corner. You're in journalism, what could happen to journalism?

Sorry, I will not confront the individual.

Because I am a doctor not a circus performer.

And that's all the time I can make right now. Poof.

(RAY, outside with his sign. His thoughts have been pent-up; he organizes them, barely, as he speaks.)

RAY. Well Tom!

I'm here to protest the telethon yes.

I feel for the sick children and their families, but Children's Hospital is not the place to give your money. I hope Doctor Kagan will accept my request for a face-to-face conversation this afternoon. There may be others attending, so get ready for a crowd.

We trusted Doctor Kagan.

She was a warm person, for a doctor.

She wore a clown nose.

That sounds real weird, almost mean, but she set us at ease.

The boys were small when we came to Children's. Seven years old.

They saw her like a mom.

The 1970s were not the ideal decade for family responsibility.

We uh we lived through a lot of changes, if you were born around 1950, hoo-boy. Evelyn and me – that's their mother – we're from Texas. You wouldn't know the town. We wanted to see California, the fruits and the nuts, that was us.

>   *(Little laugh.)*

The first time Ray Ray banged his knee and his leg swelled up like a prickly pear, Evie *[EH-vee]* knew to go right to the ER. When Mikey was diagnosed, Evie skipped to Hawaii. Her brother had it, so she thought she knew what was coming.

You move to San Diego for a beautiful life.

>   *(He holds up one finger in an "excuse me a moment" gesture, turns his back.)*

FUCK FUCK FUCK FUCK FUCK.

>   *(Turns back around.)*

One of the rougher nights, Doctor Roz gave me a book, *When Bad Things Happen to Good People*.

First off it's written by this Jewish fellow, and secondly his son *died* so I'm thinking, "What's this got to do with me?" Because our kids were not dying.

I'll say that slow.

They were doing real well.

This was after the Factor VIII came on the market and I do mean market.

She promised me one hundred and forty years of my sons' combined lives.

Normal.

I hear that, I'm thinking, Evelyn is an asshole. To be so scared of blood.

I hear normal, I see my future:

    (A glorious fantasy.)

I'm dying of some shit I deserve. Lung cancer, or heart disease from too much steak. I'm ancient, my boys are old, with bellies and grey beards; their kids bring *their* kids to sing me out with the King – I do an Elvis cover band that remains very popular, fuck this alternative shit, fuck the new wave, **the entire 1980s can suck my hairy hole** – my dynasty is crossing me over with "I Can't Help Falling in Love," and in walks Evelyn, old pruny Ev and she's like, "Ray I'm sorry."

And I go, "That's okay baby. Meet your great-grandson."

Sometimes bad things happen to good people.

And you fucking happened to me.

1977

(A hospital, in memory.)

ROZ. I thought you might want this book, Ray.

RAY. Huh. The kids are good people all right.

ROZ. I meant you.

RAY. Thank you, Doctor.

ROZ. You have a lot on your shoulders as a single parent.

RAY. Thank you.

ROZ. This book is about wrestling down the illusion that we get what we deserve.

RAY. I never held that illusion.

1991

> (**RAY** *continues where he left off, trying to keep Tom's attention.*)

RAY. Bear with me, Tom. I'm getting there. Here's an example.

I learned to cook. I had to.

I cooked and Mikey and Ray Ray did the dishes.

That Ray Ray was a clown.

He didn't want to make enough trips table to sink, you know? Didn't want to make the trips drying rack to cupboard.

Not like our kitchen is large, five steps at most.

Ray Ray was king of the balancing act.

I'd be, son, make two trips and he'd be:

> (*Balancing, Ray Ray macho.*)

Pops, I got this.

He's maybe nine. And I'm going son, put the plates *down*. Make the *trips*.

Pops I got this.

And then Crash. Broken glass is a four-alarm event in our home. Two hemophiliac third-graders crouching on their chairs and I'm – It's possible I'm raising my voice.

I won't let them down off the chairs till I've swept, mopped, wiped every inch with a wet paper towel, again and again. It takes hours. We have no room for shards.

By now Ray Ray's crying, Daddy it was an accident, and I say no, you didn't *care* enough to do it *right*.

That's not an accident, son, that's NEGLIGENCE!
My twin sons were born with a debilitating blood disease requiring ongoing medical care and sustained interdependence with doctors and blood products.

Hemophilia, a bad thing, happened.

It demanded the best available medical intervention.

Instead.

Instead, my children were injected with a blood-borne plague.

Not once.

Not twice.

But up to three times a WEEK. For their entire CHILDHOOD.

That's not something that HAPPENED.

That's something she DID.

Do NOT give your money to Children's Hospital. They are liars and killers and please put that on the air.

YOU DID IT.

YOU DID IT.

DOCTOR ROZ KAGAN KILLED MY SON.

1978

*(**RAY** and **ROZ** in Roz's office. She holds a piece of pottery made by a child.)*

ROZ. It's beautiful.

RAY. It's an ashtray. Not the ideal tribute to a doctor, but that's what he made.

ROZ. I'm honored.

RAY. They have the kids do ceramics for Mother's Day.

ROZ. Oh.

RAY. Mikey sent his to Hawaii, but Ray Ray thought of you.

ROZ. Thank you.

RAY. You have kids?

ROZ. Not yet.

RAY. Not *yet*? Sorry, don't mean to suggest that you (are old) –

ROZ. We're figuring it all out.

RAY. You and your husband?

ROZ. Me and my husband.

RAY. He a doctor too?

ROZ. Yes, actually.

RAY. He move from Ohio with you?

ROZ. Yes he did.

RAY. He as smart as you?

(**ROZ** *hesitates.*)

You paused.

ROZ. I did not.

RAY. You *paused*!

ROZ. *(The ashtray.)* I will treasure this.

RAY. Now don't start smoking.

ROZ. I quit in med school.

RAY. Sensible.

ROZ. A lot of people start then. You'd be shocked.

RAY. I would not be shocked.

ROZ. Your pickup is here.

(*She indicates a medical cooler.*)

RAY. I'll get along.

ROZ. No rush. You must not get too many breaks.

RAY. Work in the morning, boys afternoon, music by night.

ROZ. Music?

RAY. Cover band, nothing too creative. A few bucks.

ROZ. Still, you must be good.

(**RAY** *shrugs.*)

What kind of music?

RAY. Golden Oldies.

ROZ. I would not have guessed that.

RAY. It was an era, it really was, I never get sick of it. Unlike this disco business.

ROZ. I'm with you there.

*(**RAY** is about to leave.)*

RAY. You ever hear the term hemo-homo?

ROZ. Did someone tease your boys?

RAY. No, but Evie said kids used to pick on her brother.

ROZ. It was different, even ten, twenty years ago.

RAY. Why did they say that? Hemo-*homo*?

ROZ. Before Factor, it used to be that hemophiliacs couldn't run, or even really walk. They remained dependent at home. Most were on crutches by ten, in wheelchairs by twenty, died before thirty.

RAY. That was Michael, rest in peace.

ROZ. So physically, their muscles –

RAY. Soft.

ROZ. Yes. And socially –

RAY. Separate.

ROZ. Sure.

RAY. Probably crying all the fucking time. Excuse me.

ROZ. There was a fair bit of that. Also the disease only affects males, so it was an image.

RAY. I want tough guys. Run hard. Play ball.

ROZ. You got one in Ray Ray. If you're concerned, we have a social worker on staff now, Marie. I hired her.

RAY. I don't mean to take up your time with feelings.

ROZ. No, ask me, tell me. I just want you to know the resources. I don't meet many fathers in your position. I admire your strength.

RAY. I come from a line of healthy people, Doctor Roz.
I ran track back in Texas. And in the service, whoo they work you. Body a temple, you don't poison it, you push it.
My father taught me count on no one but yourself.
Yet here are my sons.
(The cooler.) Receiving in their need.
What a blessing, in its way. Everyone inside everyone else. I like that.

ROZ. I like it too.

RAY. Do you do the Red Cross drive?

ROZ. Sure, every three months.

RAY. *That* is civilization. My dad wants to talk about Jesus? A blood drive is Christ. Healthy people give to the sick, from their veins. My sons brim with the blood of the world.

ROZ. Actually, Factor doesn't come from the blood bank.

RAY. I thought Factor comes from cryo which comes from blood.

ROZ. Yes and no. Both are blood products, but – Think of a pitcher of orange juice.

RAY. Okay.

ROZ. Let's say you have your pitcher of juice but you need just the vitamin C. Making cryo is like starting with juice, separating out the water, and using the concentrate.

RAY. Okay.

ROZ. Which was a breakthrough thirty years ago, because instead of transfusing a hemophiliac with whole blood –

RAY. Gallons of juice –

ROZ. Right, doctors could give them cryo.

RAY. Less juice, same vitamin C. I follow you.

ROZ. Which was better, but severe hemophiliacs need a lot of cryo per transfusion.

RAY. I remember. Ten bags at a time. All day in the hospital.

ROZ. Now, imagine if you could take that pitcher of orange juice and extract the pure vitamin C. That's what these commercial labs do today, when they make Factor.

RAY. So if cryo is the can of concentrate, Factor is a vitamin pill.

ROZ. Exactly! *And* whereas cryo relied on volunteer blood donation so was always in short supply, these new commercial labs have the technology to collect blood, remove the liquid that contains Factor, and reinfuse the donor with his own red blood cells. So he can donate more often, a couple times a week instead of every three months. They become like professionals.

RAY. Paid?

ROZ. Yes, I believe they are paid.

RAY. Who are these professionals?

ROZ. *(She really doesn't know and is unworried.)* I don't know. We buy it from Baxter Pharmaceuticals.

RAY. Well bless them whoever they are.

ROZ. Yes, there's no going back to the Dark Ages.

RAY. Weeks in the hospital, uh-uh. I'd rather pick up the Factor while Ray Ray plays ball.

ROZ. That's right.

RAY. *(The cooler.)* Do I sign for this?

ROZ. Joanne will help you at the front desk.

RAY. Doctor Roz. You have worked a miracle in my home.

ROZ. I entered the field at the right time, when we have a good product, that's all.

RAY. That's not all. You actually care.

(He leaves. ROZ holds her ashtray.)

1991

(Same day. ROZ answers the phone in her office. We hear a bit of RAY's chant outside: "Doctor Roz Kagan killed my son.")

ROZ. Yeah Tom. You're having a good day huh? My worst day is your best day, that's why we're close.

He sounds personal, you noticed? Why would Ray Leon sound so personal?

Okay, lemme give you a for instance: When I began my career, hemophilia care was brutal. My first rotation in the ER, I'm a wide-eyed doe of a thing – this was a couple centuries ago – the ambulance brings in a child screaming, thrashing. My first hemophiliac.

They strapped him to a board to keep him still for a transfusion.

I said this is a chronic disease, why is he being seen in the ER? And the attending doc says, "Fucking hemos, they're like fire drills, just get it done fast."

And I thought: no.

I will change this.

Children will not be afraid. They will understand their care.

Not because I'm female, Tom, but because I'm human.

I was way ahead of the curve; I brought new protocol to San Diego Children's. My mentor didn't believe little guys could handle a needle; I said tell you what, they can practice on me.

You want to talk about skin in the game? Every one of my patients stuck a needle in my arm. I rolled up my sleeve and *made it personal*.

Plus, we didn't let them go. Remember most hemophiliacs used to die in childhood, so only pediatricians learned their care. When our young adults tried to see regular internists, bad things happened.

So we let them stay with us at Children's. Informally. They were our long-term cheerful success stories. We went to weddings and met babies. We grew up together. It was fun.

1980

(A snatch of children's Christmas music [e.g. Alvin and the Chipmunks].* A big Santa suit hangs in Roz's office, complete with red hat and beard.)

---

*A license to produce *Roz and Ray* does not include a performance license for any third-party or copyrighted music. Licensees should create an original composition or use music in the public domain. For further information, please see Music Use Note on page 3.

(**ROZ** pulls **RAY** into the office. The first time we see her out of her lab coat. She's in a state of mortal panic.)

ROZ. Ray!

RAY. Merry Christmas.

(**RAY** is amused. **ROZ** does not find this funny at all.)

ROZ. You have to be Santa!

RAY. I what?

ROZ. Doctor Lee is in surgery. He can't make the party. Be Santa.

RAY. You be Santa.

ROZ. I can't be Santa, I'm a woman.

RAY. Doctor Lee is Chinese.

ROZ. Ray I'm serious. The kids are yelling for Santa. Here's the suit.

RAY. I'll help you change.

ROZ. No no no no no. You change. Please?

RAY. The boys will recognize me.

ROZ. They'll recognize me.

RAY. They're eleven, they know there's no Santa.

ROZ. Great. So.

(She holds up the suit.)

RAY. Uh-uh.

ROZ. But you *perform*.

RAY. So can you.

ROZ. No, no. I'm shy.

(Tiny beat.)

RAY. What did Doctor Lee say?

ROZ. He left a memo with Joanne.

RAY. What did it say?

ROZ. It said, "I'm in surgery."

RAY. And?

ROZ. "I'm in surgery. Be Santa."

RAY. This is your job.

ROZ. But you would be better.

RAY. Sure I would. But your *boss* told you to be Santa.

ROZ. He doesn't care who –

RAY. *Now* you're going to tell him, "I can't, I'm a woman?" After how hard you work? How you achieved equality? Now you can't because you're a *woman*?

ROZ. *(Hoping she's right.)* It's just Santa.

RAY. Doctor Lee sees you as Santa. He didn't think twice. He said, "Be Santa." That's great! Don't get me to do it.

ROZ. But you do Elvis.

RAY. Different.

ROZ. Closer.

RAY. *Ho ho ho.*

ROZ. Come on.

RAY. Try it. *Ho ho ho.*

ROZ. I don't even celebrate Christmas.

RAY. You should come for Christmas!

ROZ. Really?

RAY. That would be fun, you and your husband right?

ROZ. He might have plans.

RAY. Okay just the four of us then, either way, or my mother might come in; I make a ham, does your faith –

ROZ. I eat ham.

RAY. Okay, oh boy, we are set. Doctor Roz is coming for Christmas!

ROZ. Terrific.

RAY. Right after you do Santa.

ROZ. I get stage fright.

RAY. Just think: I have what you want.

ROZ. I have what you want?

RAY. I have what you want.

ROZ. I have what you want.

RAY. *(Like Santa.)* I have what you want for CHRISTMAS.
ROZ. Ray –
RAY. Ho ho ho!
ROZ. *(Not even trying.)* Ho ho ho.
RAY. Lower. Ho ho ho!
ROZ. *(Trying a little.)* Ho ho ho!
RAY. Louder. Ho ho ho!
ROZ. *(Trying, still terrible.)* Ho ho ho!
RAY. Good, let's try the beard.
ROZ. No one will believe me.
RAY. The little ones will believe you and the big ones already know.

> *(**RAY** places the beard and hat on her, adjusting gently. It's intimate.)*

You are going to be the best Santa Claus the Children's Hospital Hematology-Oncology Unit ever saw.
ROZ. Come on.
RAY. You know why? Because you're real.
ROZ. Ray.
RAY. You *do* have what we need. You *do* go child to child. You *do* pull each one close and ask questions. What do you want for Christmas?
ROZ. I don't even (celebrate)…
RAY. *(Santa.)* What do you want for Christmas?
ROZ. *(Attempt at Santa.)* What do you want for Christmas?
RAY. *(Santa.)* What do you want for Christmas?
ROZ. *(Attempt at Santa.)* What do you want for Christmas?
RAY. Ho ho ho!
ROZ. Ho ho ho!
RAY. Better. Ho ho ho!
ROZ. Ho ho ho!
RAY. Ho ho ho what do you want for CHRISTMAS?
ROZ. Ho ho ho what do you want for CHRISTMAS?
RAY. Get that suit on girl because you are SANTA.

ROZ. I'm Santa!

RAY. You want privacy?

ROZ. Just help me.

>*(He helps her put on the Santa jacket.)*

I'm Santa. I'm Santa.

RAY. You're Santa.

ROZ. I'm Santa.

>*(Best yet.)* **Ho ho ho what do you want for CHRISTMAS?**

RAY. Go get 'em.

1982

>*(Club music.*)*
>
>*(A phone rings very loudly in Roz's home.* **ROZ** *answers, energized.)*

ROZ. This is Doctor Kagan.

>*(**RAY** is panicked. We might see club lights.)*

RAY. It's Ray Ray!

ROZ. Start at the start.

RAY. I should *not* have gone *out*.

ROZ. Where are you, Ray?

RAY. I called Mikey. He said Ray Ray had a headache, fell asleep and won't wake up.

ROZ. I see.

RAY. I should NOT have gone OUT.

ROZ. Did Mikey try water –

RAY. Water, ice, a slap on the wrist –

---

*A license to produce *Roz and Ray* does not include a performance license for any third-party or copyrighted music. Licensees should create an original composition or use music in the public domain. For further information, please see Music Use Note on page 3.

ROZ. Can Mikey stay alone while the ambulance brings Ray / Ray to the emergency –

RAY. I should NOT have gone OUT.

ROZ. Call 9-1-1. Make sure they go to Children's –

RAY. I should not have / done that.

ROZ. They'll want to route him to Edgemoor but there's no hemophilia care. Tell them Children's.

RAY. I can't tell an *ambulance* where to –

ROZ. I'll meet you there.

RAY. You will?

> *(Lights out on **RAY**. **ROZ** yells on the phone as she prepares herself:)*

ROZ. 9-1-1. You have an incoming medical call for Leon in Santee?

Do not route the patient to Edgemoor. Take patient to Children's Hospital in San Diego. Patient is a pediatric hemophiliac and needs specialty care.

It could be spontaneous intracranial bleeding.

I am not a nurse I am his doctor.

YES DO CONNECT ME WITH YOUR FUCKING –

(To supervisor.) Hello this is Doctor Rosalyn Kagan – Please take pediatric patient Raymond Leon Jr. to Children's Hospital.

I'll handle billing.

I'll bring the supplies.

Sir, I am recording this call.

The child could die or suffer permanent brain damage, in which case my legal department will be up your ass so high we jump out your throat. **GET HIM TO CHILDREN'S.**

> *(Same night. Children's ER waiting room, maybe an animal mural. **RAY** paces. He wears something that a gay man would wear clubbing at the time [i.e. a leather vest]. The clothing outs him unmistakably without being too distracting.)*

*(**ROZ** barrels in carrying two medical coolers.)*

RAY. They won't start surgery without the –

ROZ. I have the Factor.

RAY. That's good.

*(**ROZ** blows past **RAY** into surgery. He holds an unlit cigarette in his palm. He paces alone.)*

*(**ROZ** emerges.)*

Will Ray Ray be okay?

ROZ. They're looking for a head bleed.

RAY. I should NOT have gone out.

*(**RAY** paces. **ROZ** takes in his clothes.)*

ROZ. What are you – were you with your band?

*(A moment of **RAY** feeling exposed.)*

RAY. Yeah.

You got here quick.

ROZ. I was up.

RAY. Huh.

Do you help with the surgery, or?

ROZ. Nope. I called in a neurosurgeon.

RAY. You did?

ROZ. That's what he needs. Injections are about as far as my butterfingers go. But I can peek in on him for you.

RAY. That would be...

*(**ROZ** leaves. **RAY** prays alone.)*

RAY. I have no right.
To pray to you.
I'm a sinner.
I'm a sinner.
But Ray Ray did no harm.
For him.
For him I pray.
In Jesus' name.

(**ROZ** *re-enters.*)

ROZ. The surgeon found the bleed. They're infusing the Factor. They'll be ready to operate as soon as the clotting agent permeates his blood.

RAY. Will he be okay?

ROZ. The bleed looks moderate. It's well-contained. They got him here in time. Ray Ray's oxygen levels stayed normal so he should recover fully.

RAY. Thank you! Oh god! Thank you for getting us to Children's. Thank you for calling the neurosurgeon. I don't know how you did that.

ROZ. Job description.

RAY. You should get some rest.

ROZ. I'll wait with you.

(**ROZ** *sits near* **RAY**.)

RAY. You would make a great mom.

ROZ. Jesus, Ray.

RAY. Now I scared you off.

ROZ. No.

RAY. You're still married, right?

ROZ. The advantage of "Doctor." You don't have to broadcast your business, and you don't piss anyone off using "Ms."

(**RAY***'s unlit cigarette is mangled in his fingers by now.*)

Are you going to smoke that?

RAY. Do you want me to, *Doctor*?

ROZ. I'm feeling sorry for your cigarette.

RAY. They changed the rules since last time. No smoking in the waiting room.

ROZ. Tough break.

RAY. Wouldn't you approve?

ROZ. People need their vices.

RAY. You used to wear a ring.

ROZ. He and I wanted the same thing.

RAY. What's that?

ROZ. A wife.

RAY. Oh!

ROZ. I don't mean –

RAY. Sure.

ROZ. An individual to defrost the chicken, sort the mail.
I've been told I leave my nurturing instincts at the office.

RAY. What happens to your mail?

ROZ. The mail will wait.
That's mail with an "I." The male with an "E" loses patience and returns to Ohio.

RAY. His loss.

ROZ. Thanks.

RAY. I should not have gone out.

ROZ. No blame game.

> *(He takes her hand.)*

RAY. I should have stayed home.
I should not have been doing that.

ROZ. Whatever you did, it's okay.

RAY. I called you so late.

ROZ. I'm glad to help.
(A confession.) I was glad to get your call.

RAY. *(Gazing into her eyes.)* What would I do without you?

> *(**ROZ** kisses **RAY**. The kiss develops for a while and looks mutual, but **ROZ** is hungrier. Eventually **ROZ** realizes **RAY** isn't returning full-force, and she ends the kiss.)*

ROZ. Oh god.

RAY. You're so kind.

ROZ. Oh shit.

RAY. Smooth move, Raymond.

ROZ. No –

RAY. I let you walk right into that.

ROZ. Under no circumstance should I have –

RAY. We need you.

ROZ. Ray I love your kids. I'm the asshole to cross that line.

RAY. If I'm your Saturday night date what can I expect?

ROZ. Boundaries?

RAY. If you had boundaries you wouldn't answer the phone at midnight.

ROZ. I was up.

RAY. If you had boundaries I wouldn't know your home number. If you had boundaries my sons would have died. Probably a dozen times.

ROZ. I love those boys.

RAY. I love them too.

(She takes him in, club clothes and all.)

ROZ. Are you gay?

RAY. I have two sons.

ROZ. I know...

RAY. Come here.

(He holds her. She's unnerved. She is in love with him. Every cell in her body wants him.)

ROZ. I'll refer you to Doctor Morada.

RAY. No you will not.

ROZ. I don't know if I'm capable of making unbiased decisions for you and your boys.

RAY. Good. You're on our side. More than a doctor. Above and beyond, right?

ROZ. Always. But that's not / how it works.

RAY. Let me buy you some breakfast.

ROZ. He'll be out soon.

RAY. Just in the cafeteria.

ROZ. That's probably okay.

RAY. I appreciate you. So much.

ROZ. You know what, don't embarrass me.

RAY. Off base in Pleiku I wanted a tattoo: Love is not shame. But the guy didn't speak English and I thought he might mess up the writing. Which would defeat the purpose.

(**RAY** *is still holding* **ROZ.**)

ROZ. Were you intending a military career?

RAY. Just the college money. Still untapped.

ROZ. Fantastic! Where will you –

RAY. Ah fuck I didn't want to tell you because I knew you'd be on me to go.

ROZ. You bet I will.

RAY. Why medicine?

ROZ. Good at science.

RAY. Why not nursing, or teaching?

ROZ. Very good at science.

RAY. How does a girl of – how old were you when you chose?

ROZ. Twelve.

RAY. How does a girl of twelve learn that she is very good at science?

ROZ. My dad.

RAY. Doctor dad!

ROZ. Sick dad.

RAY. Poor kid.

ROZ. *(Shrugs.)* My parents didn't speak perfect English, and the doctors explained everything in medical jargon, if they explained at all. So I looked up terms. I read his charts. My mother bought me a stethoscope. I listened to his heart.

RAY. Hell of a science lesson.

ROZ. It was a long time ago.

RAY. Poor little – were you Kagan?

ROZ. Yeah.

RAY. Poor little Roz Kagan.

ROZ. Rosie.

RAY. Rosie. Thank you for that.

ROZ. You're welcome.

RAY. Poor little Rosie Kagan.

ROZ. Everybody lied. They said he'd be fine. He was not fine. He said, don't let me die alone in a hospital; guess what, he died alone in the hospital.

RAY. I just want to kiss your little broken heart.

ROZ. You're doing pretty well.

RAY. I said appreciate but I mean, I love you. We all do.

ROZ. That's okay.

RAY. Do you want that breakfast?

ROZ. I'm not hungry. I'd better go.

RAY. *(Sexual.)* Be with me.

> *(Pause.)*

ROZ. I hope your kids will stay healthy, and we will see each other less.

RAY. I hope half of that.

ROZ. I'll call the hospital to check on Ray Ray. I'm glad for any help I could provide. Good night.

RAY. When can I see you?

> *(**ROZ** gives **RAY** a key.)*

Your home?

ROZ. I just, I live much closer, you're all the way out in Santee, and so if you need to, after your band or –

RAY. For convenience.

ROZ. Under extreme circumstances, there can arise a form of…battle heat.

RAY. People meet in many ways, many combinations.

ROZ. You were in a war; you know battle heat.

RAY. I was a medic. I didn't kill anyone.

ROZ. You didn't say you were a *medic*. That's lovely.

RAY. Yes, I'm lovely.

ROZ. Shit!

RAY. What is wrong with you?

ROZ. A lot is probably wrong with me, obviously.

RAY. Obviously because of me?

ROZ. Not you. The category of you.

RAY. What category is that?

ROZ. You're the father of my patients...

RAY. I know that part.

ROZ. And I don't understand...what type of man you are.

RAY. What's my category.

ROZ. Yeah.

RAY. What's your category?

ROZ. My category?

RAY. We are people. Human souls and bodies. You heal my children; to me that's a plus. I want to heal you back a little. Will you let me?

ROZ. *(With all her willpower.)* Not tonight.

RAY. You want your key back?

ROZ. Keep it.

(She goes.)

1991

(Same day.)

RAY. It wasn't until much later that I learned everyone involved was making big bucks off the Factor VIII, including Children's Hospital.

In the early 1980s this broker came to San Diego and was trying to permeate the hemophilia population locally so he could sell us the Factor. He was a hemophiliac too. He came to me and asked if I wanted to start utilizing his services. And I can't believe I said this but I did: "Well let me talk to Doctor Kagan because they have taken care of us so well I want to see what she says."

That is how badly I misunderstood the situation. That is how much I trusted her.

We're fucked. There is no nicer way to say it.

She is a killer and when I see her I will tell her to her face.

1982

(Very early morning, a few days after the hospital scene. **RAY** *finds* **ROZ** *in her office, absorbed in work. He's romantic.)*

RAY. Good morning.

Earth to Roz?

  *(**ROZ** startles.)*

ROZ. Hi, Ray.

RAY. I woke up in your bed and you weren't there.

ROZ. *(Smiles.)* No, I'm here.

RAY. Why?

ROZ. Reading.

  *(**RAY** rubs **ROZ**'s shoulders.)*

RAY. Reading?

ROZ. That feels so good.

RAY. Marry me.

ROZ. Jesus, Ray.

  (He touches her in a small, electric way.)

RAY. This worked.

ROZ. It sure did.

RAY. So everything is simple.

ROZ. Ray. It's getting scary.

RAY. I'm harmless.

ROZ. I'm scared for the kids.

RAY. Let's tell the kids. Let's be a family.

ROZ. This bug.

RAY. What bug?

ROZ. I don't like the contagion pattern.

RAY. The gay bug?

ROZ. Yeah.

RAY. Why are you reading about the gay bug after our very / first…

ROZ. If it spreads the same way as Hepatitis B, which it might, then it is not only sexually transmitted but blood-borne, and will reach the same populations as Hep B.

> *(Most of **ROZ**'s attention stays with the journals, trying to work through the problem.)*

RAY. My boys both had Hep B.

ROZ. Yes. It's a risk of pooled blood products but Hep B is a prudent risk. It's treatable. As this bug is expected to be treatable. It is expected that most patients will carry it and clear it, very few will succumb. It is predicted to be a manageable disease, like Hep B.

RAY. Are you saying no panic.

ROZ. There is no general panic.

RAY. But?

ROZ. But I don't like it. There have been two hemophiliac deaths. Why did they die? Is that two out of a hundred cases or two out of two?

RAY. What will you do?

ROZ. I'm a hematologist-oncologist not an epidemiologist.

RAY. Um what?

ROZ. I treat what presents. I'm not an authority on how it spreads.

RAY. What do the authorities say?

ROZ. Split. The Center for Disease Control flagged these two cases as a possible pandemic, but the National Hemophilia Foundation won't change protocol without more data.

RAY. And you're a hematologist so you keep protocol?

ROZ. Two deaths, eight reported cases; from a medical standpoint it's insignificant. But from an epidemiological perspective – which is not my field – that's how...

RAY. That's how what.

ROZ. I'm just reading two sets of journals side by side, there must be experts studying this, I'm practically a layman. I have a bad feeling. But who am I?

RAY. You? Are the smartest person I know. You know and I know you had to be twice as good as the other docs. They are home with their wives right now and here's Roz the one night she got lucky. You look like shit.

ROZ. Thanks.

RAY. You don't sleep. You don't cook. You probably never see the beach.

ROZ. San Diego has a beach?

RAY. You live on junk. You take too many pills. I think you're smoking again.

ROZ. So?

RAY. You give it your all, Roz Kagan, until there's nothing left.

ROZ. I'm sorry.

RAY. Don't apologize. Get your act together and stand up for my kids.

ROZ. Well. One doctor in Philadelphia – one – is insisting his patients go back to cryoprecipitate.

RAY. Cryo? The transfusions?

ROZ. He won't give Factor anymore. He's sticking with his local blood bank, taking hemophilia care back twenty years. They're calling him a dinosaur.

RAY. Sure.

ROZ. Do I want that? Would I take away everything your kids can do, their health, their whole lives, because of a hunch?

RAY. It's not *a* hunch, it's *your* hunch. And at least one guy in Philly has the same hunch.

ROZ. He's a senior doc; he runs that practice. I'm low on the totem pole.

RAY. So?

ROZ. I'd have to convince the whole department, starting with Doctor Lee.

RAY. Okay, I'm Doctor Lee. You be you. What do you say?

> *(Beat.)*

ROZ. I might say, "Phillip. There are eight hemophiliacs in the United States presenting symptoms of Gay-Related Immune Deficiency. Two have died. While that is not even a tiny fraction of the hemophiliacs in this country, I am worried –" I can't say worried.

RAY. Why not?

ROZ. It's a feeling word.

RAY. Doctors are weird.

ROZ. Yeah.

"The Center for Disease Control hypothesizes that these cases were contracted from commercial blood products. I suggest we break with the National Hemophilia Foundation and cease treatment with Factor VIII, now."

RAY. And he says?

ROZ. "What do we give our patients instead?"

RAY. And you say –

ROZ. "Cryo."

RAY. *(As himself.) Cryo?*

ROZ. And he says:

"Do you suggest that we withhold a miraculous product that sustains these children's normal lifestyles, to reintroduce a painful and ineffective treatment that will leave some of them crippled?"

RAY. Hmm. And you say:

ROZ. "Yes. Yes I do." And he says, "Why?" And I say, "Because I have a feeling –" not feeling – I say, "Because there's a chance, a tiny chance, that this bug could be worse."

RAY. Worse.

ROZ. So he says, "Worse than the debilitating symptoms of juvenile hemophilia unchecked by Factor? Do you remember the history of this disease?"

I say of course I remember, but I feel, no I think, I –

He says, "Families will leave. They will go to Los Angeles to get Factor. Two hundred miles round-trip is easier than the cryo."

He says, "I brought you here to start a state-of-the-art medical practice. If our patients leave, what's your practice?

The National Hemophilia Foundation follows protocol but Roz Kagan follows her *feminine intuition*."

Do you know how many women were in the University of Cincinnati School of Medicine class of 1966?

RAY. One?

ROZ. Three. But I'm the only one who specialized. I'm the only one who opened a practice. I'm the only one here. If I'm wrong...

   (A decision.)

I can't do it. I don't have the numbers. I don't have a tolerable alternate plan of care. I don't have anything to offer.

RAY. You will figure this out.

ROZ. Ray. Use condoms.

RAY. We did.

ROZ. Out there.

RAY. You think I have a lot of free time.

ROZ. Ray don't joke.

RAY. You think that's what I meant by marry me? Me and you and "out there"?

ROZ. I don't know.

RAY. I mean family. Be my family.

ROZ. I think I need to be the doctor. Not more. Not less.

RAY. Deal.

>   (**ROZ** *is heartbroken.*)

ROZ. Deal.

RAY. *(Not unkind.)* Am I supposed to say something else?

ROZ. No. No you're perfect. I screw everything up. I'm sorry.

RAY. Uh-uh. Ray is in charge of Ray.

ROZ. I don't know how to be close, or when, when to be close. I don't know when to be difficult, when to make a scene, when to keep my mouth shut, how to see what's right in front of me. I wanted to be a different kind of doctor.

RAY. You are.

ROZ. *(Their relationship.)* This was not what I had in mind.

RAY. Forget it.

ROZ. Thank you for even… I've been told I'm a tough… I'm probably just not –

RAY. Roz.

>   *(He kisses her lightly.)*

There is nothing wrong with you.

>   (**ROZ** *takes in this possibility, maybe for the first time.*)

ROZ. Ditto.

RAY. You have a nice house. You should go there more often.

ROZ. Yeah I'll try that.

RAY. Are you okay?

ROZ. Oh god, I'm great! You should not be worried about me! You of all people.

RAY. You will fight for those boys. I know you.

ROZ. I'd better start my day.

RAY. Should I pick up the Factor while I'm here?

ROZ. Might as well. The new batch is in the fridge. Joanne isn't in yet. I'll sign for you.

RAY. Thanks.

ROZ. You bet, Ray.

> (**RAY** *exits.* **ROZ** *jerks herself into action for the day.*)

1991

RAY. Every word that came out of her mouth was very measured because she supposedly didn't know what was going on either. Now I see this isn't true.

Certain people knew in 1983 that there was a problem with the Factor. The Cutter memo proves that. Cutter is one of the companies that manufactures blood products, and they had a legal memo in hand in *1983* that said, "There's a large potential problem here; we should put in a warning label and an instruction sheet to the doctors, stating that the Factor could be contaminated." But Cutter fought the *warning label* for two years.

"We didn't know." That's how they all do it. That's how the pharmaceutical people do it, that's how the blood bank does it, the medical enterprise in total, down to Roz Kagan. That's the whole defense. Well I don't accept it.

It was her job to know.

Furthermore she did know.

Blood for money and money for blood. They swapped.

1984

> (*A hospital meeting room.* **ROZ** *addresses about fifty people.*)

ROZ. Ricky would you mind joining Marie outside; this talk is just for parents and the patients over twelve.

*(A little pause. **ROZ** is good at this.)*

ROZ. Gentlemen. I've known some of you guys since you were babies; it's awkward. But here we go: If you are sexually active or even sexually hopeful, you need one of these.

(A condom.)

Even if you're married – congratulations James. Go ahead, laugh. But let's control what we can control here. And sexual behavior, despite rumors to the contrary, can be controlled!

Now. Regarding the Factor VIII.

We don't need to panic. But if you are taking Factor regularly to prevent bleeding, don't do that anymore.

A new heat-treated Factor developed in Germany is now available in the US. Heat seems to kill the AIDS virus. It's considered experimental, as there is still no reliable test. But here at Children's we will switch to the heat-treated Factor now; we will not wait for guidelines from the National Hemophilia Foundation.

I urge you to discard whatever supplies you have at home. We don't know which lots are bad. I realize there is a cost. We are working with our pharmaceutical suppliers on a buy-back, a formal recall. That's been slow.

Meanwhile it is an option to go back to cryoprecipitate. That would mean that in case of a bleed you would come to the hospital for a transfusion, rather than treating at home.

We held a regional meeting, LA Children's, LA Orthopedic, San Diego Children's. We reached a consensus. Adopt the heat-treated Factor, but wait for a bleed. Use less.

Marie is available if anyone wants to talk.

This is somber and upsetting news. But let's not panic.

*(She gathers her things. A sense that the room is clearing out. **RAY** approaches her.)*

RAY. That was on message.
ROZ. It's good to see you.
RAY. Consensus, huh?
ROZ. As a smaller clinic it makes sense for us to work in step with the other programs.
RAY. You can't test for this?
ROZ. Center for Disease Control is working on a test.
RAY. It's been two years.
ROZ. There's no money for research. There is nothing. The president has not said the word AIDS.
RAY. No one gives a shit about the gays.
ROZ. I go over and over this with my colleagues in LA. I'm up all night.
RAY. If you were their mom what would you do?
ROZ. I would treat for the bleed. With heat-treated Factor VIII. The trials look very good.
RAY. What about cryo?
ROZ. We can make that available to you.
RAY. But you said a long time ago there isn't enough to go around.
ROZ. Sure if everyone went back on the cryo we'd have a supply problem. But that's unlikely because it's inconvenient.
RAY. If my kids want cryo there is cryo for us?
ROZ. Yes.
RAY. And it's safer?
ROZ. Well, the odds are better. Fewer donors per bag.
RAY. It's from our local Red Cross.
ROZ. Should be.
RAY. I still donate every three months. Least I can do.
ROZ. Ray, if you're sleeping with men you should stop donating blood.
RAY. Wow you just want to be in every part of my business.
ROZ. It's common sense. I'm not sure why the gay leaders haven't been more emphatic on this point.

RAY. I don't know the GAY LEADERS, Roz.

I hang out here. In the hospital. In these waiting rooms listening to the other parents whose sons have been STRUCK LIKE MINE, who want to put the faggots in concentration camps. Blame the queers for the dirty blood. I hear this EVERY TIME I WAIT WITH MY KIDS. That our boys are the innocent victims. The poor Ryan White kid kicked out of school. Innocent. I hear ENOUGH ABOUT FAGGOTS POISONING THE BLOOD.

ROZ. Okay.

RAY. I will tell you something else, Doctor Roz.

The nice buttfucker piano teacher donors are probably safer. Than the "professionals" who sold their blood off the street?

That's the poison.

I'm reading up.

Blood the source of life was bought and sold. Bought from junkies and hookers and prisoners. Sold to Cutter, Baxter, Bayer, et cetera. Repackaged and resold to me, to my children.

The poison is cash.

Don't blame the faggots for participating in the gift of blood donation.

Don't blame the faggots for participating in civilization as is our their RIGHT.

ROZ. I see your point Ray but if you belong to a risk group –

RAY. Plus I barely have sex!

And when I do I heed your doctorly advice about the rubbers.

ROZ. Good.

RAY. Oh it's great.

ROZ. The gay community is doing almost all the work on this, all the advocacy.

RAY. I see those freaks. Acting up.

ROZ. Our kids have the potential to shift public sympathy. If hemophiliacs and their families can join the larger movement, we might be able to speed up the research.

RAY. I'm not going to handcuff myself to a blood bank in San Francisco.

ROZ. That's where the main effort –

RAY. *(End of conversation.)* I don't have the time.

My boys are fifteen. They're just starting out.

ROZ. I missed Ray Ray at the meeting.

RAY. He has a game.

ROZ. Great, but he needs to understand sexual transmission.

RAY. You ever try to control a boy who's fifteen?

ROZ. All the time.

RAY. The kid's on the bench these days, still yells his head off. Mikey's in band.

ROZ. Wonderful.

RAY. Trumpet.

ROZ. Fantastic.

RAY. I've been listening to him practice five years and I'm just now able to stand it. A lot of potential, my kids. All potential.

ROZ. We can switch them to cryo. Or the heat-treated Factor looks good.

RAY. Insurance charges us double for the heat-treated.

ROZ. Is that right?

RAY. One of the Hemophilia Chapter guys says he can sell it to us cheaper.

ROZ. I would prefer you buy from the hospital.

RAY. Gotta make that buck.

ROZ. It's an issue of medical control. Though the Factor sales do give us a tiny bit of clout.

RAY. Uh-huh.

ROZ. Children's wants to close the hemophilia clinic. Send you up to LA.

RAY. Motherfuckers.

ROZ. We run at a loss.

RAY. You're telling me.

ROZ. It's all moving to a new model. The HMOs. The for-profit hospitals. Partnerships with the big pharma companies.

RAY. Fucking Reagan.

ROZ. Fucking Reagan. Everything's supposed to run in the black.

RAY. Sick kids don't run in the black.

ROZ. We're on the same side.

RAY. My boys got taller than me.

ROZ. I know. I don't even do their physicals anymore because they're young men.

RAY. They are so close. So close to grown.

ROZ. I've known all of these guys since they were small.

RAY. Promise me you'll get them there.

ROZ. All I can tell you is the truth.

RAY. *(Turns his back.)* Fuck fuck fuck fuck fuck.

ROZ. Come here. Can I?

RAY. Fuck fuck fuck fuck fuck.

>   (**ROZ** *physically comforts* **RAY** *in a doctor/patient way.*)

We should put them on the cryo.

ROZ. Fine.

RAY. But then they're hemo-homos again. The bruising, the bleeding, the hospital.

ROZ. I know.

RAY. Maybe just for a time, till you have a test.

ROZ. We can try it.

RAY. They've been on the Factor eight years. How many vials?

ROZ. Thousands.

RAY. How many donors per vial?

ROZ. Sixty thousand.

(*Silence.*)

RAY. They all have it already, don't they?

ROZ. There is no reliable test.

RAY. What's your gut?

(**ROZ** *can't answer.*)

What's your advice?

ROZ. Stay with the heat-treated Factor VIII.

RAY. That's what we'll do.

ROZ. Continue to buy from Children's? At least I know our supplier.

RAY. Okay.

ROZ. It's an issue of medical control.

RAY. You have everything under control?

ROZ. I'm trying.

RAY. I trust you.

1991

RAY. In 1985 she secretly tested the boys for HIV. She never told them and she never told the families. It was all done underhanded. The only reason I found out was because in 1987 another boy with hemophilia saw results of that 1985 test in his own records, with everybody's name, and Mikey's name was negative. Of course by 1987, over ninety percent of the hemophiliacs in this country were positive.

ROZ. You want to know about *nineteen eighty fucking five*? Fine. In 1985, just prior to the development of a reliable test for the AIDS virus, I got a call from a colleague in research, "I have an investigational test kit for HTLV-3. I would like some specimen to test." I said okay. We sent blood samples and he sent results back in an informal, collegial way, and we put it in each patient's chart. For better or worse that's how we did it. Mikey came back negative on that test.

On that test also was a girl, not a hemophiliac, a transplant patient. She was clearly dying of AIDS. And her test was negative. So we retested her sample. Again, negative.

Huh.

I knew that child had AIDS. She was wasting away.

So here I was with a test that was unproven, and which I knew had missed this patient.

What would you do?

Even if it was a good test, let's imagine it was reliable. What would one do in 1985 for a hemophiliac with a negative HIV test? Keep him on the best product available. And the best product available was heat-treated Factor VIII. By then we knew the heat treatment worked.

So that's what we did for Mikey.

And that's what we did for the positive ones too.

We weren't testing the patients. We were testing the test.

1987

(Roz's office. **RAY** *enters, out of breath.)*

RAY. Sorry we're late. Ray Ray needed a hand. Mikey's got him.

ROZ. Are you okay?

RAY. I ran from the parking lot. Ray Ray's had the flu, it isn't too bad today, but he's moving a little slow. Then I forgot about the new office...

I don't think I was ever late, all these years.

ROZ. I think you're right. Catch your breath.

RAY. The boys can drive, but I want to be part of the consultation. Since you got Mikey's results back.

ROZ. Yes, we tested at the patient's request.

RAY. Well?

ROZ. Your son is eighteen, so I need to speak to the patient himself.

RAY. Of course we have to play by the rules.

ROZ. The new anonymity laws are serious, Ray. I can lose my license for even noting a patient was tested.

RAY. I understand the HIV test was a formality, more or less, at this point?

ROZ. *(Delicate.)* It was.

>   (**RAY** *is crushed.*)

RAY. I knew that.
It's just that Mikey is so strong, he's filled out so much you wouldn't believe it even the last six months. Eighteen years old.

ROZ. We should discuss that.

RAY. You take a look at that big lunk and then we'll discuss it!

ROZ. Michael and Raymond are adults.

RAY. Thanks to you. You're a good doctor.

ROZ. This is a children's hospital.

RAY. Why are you telling me things I already know?

ROZ. They need to be seen with other adults.

RAY. The hemophiliacs don't age out. We went over this years ago. They stay under your care.

ROZ. That was the informal system. But we are a children's hospital. We don't have an AIDS ward –

RAY. Ward?

ROZ. I mean we don't have the expertise. We are not the best facility.

RAY. But you know us.

ROZ. The decision now is whether to continue this warm relationship or find your sons the most advanced medical care.

RAY. You're dumping / them –

ROZ. I am moving / them –

RAY. – because of the HIV.

ROZ. – because they are adults.

RAY. Where will we go?

ROZ. To University Hospital.

RAY. University? That's not a hospital it's a city.

ROZ. It's the best local hospital for AIDS research.

RAY. What about hemophilia care?

ROZ. I am in touch with the staff over there. I'm sending all the information.

RAY. So it's done.

ROZ. It will be a transition. It may take about a year to cross the adult / patients over.

RAY. Can you promise a year?

ROZ. The timeline also depends on what your sons need.

RAY. They need you. You're supposed to support the family, treat them like people. Be a different kind of doctor.

ROZ. I have to take emotions out of the picture. Ray Ray's care is complicated. Mikey's care could get there too.

RAY. So you dump us. It's over.

ROZ. There is a lot being done right now.

RAY. "There is a lot being done right now." You sound like a pamphlet.

ROZ. I am not an AIDS doctor.

RAY. No one's an AIDS doctor, right? This thing is only a few years old. You're all learning as you go, that's what you said.

ROZ. I can't focus on this properly. I can't keep up with the research. Over at University they're seeing case after case. Building the science.

RAY. You're good at science.

ROZ. Most of my patients have childhood cancer, Ray. What about them?

RAY. What about Mikey and Ray Ray?

ROZ. Michael and Raymond are adults.

RAY. They have zits. They have terrible judgment. Ray Ray's still setting his farts on fire.

ROZ. You're kidding me.

RAY. I wish I was.

ROZ. Well. If childish behavior qualified you for Children's Hospital, we'd need a lot more beds.

RAY. Good one, Roz.

ROZ. Raymond is an adult AIDS patient. Michael is an HIV-positive adult.

RAY. He wasn't positive two years ago.

ROZ. Ray we went over this.

RAY. That test was negative.

ROZ. Now with a reliable test they're finding batches of contaminated Factor dating back to the seventies.

RAY. What about the children with AIDS? You hanging on to them?

ROZ. They have nowhere else to go. Your sons have an alternative.

RAY. It's a maze over at University. It's a zoo. You're throwing them in with all kinds of...AIDS people.

ROZ. What's your support system?

RAY. I'll talk to Marie.

ROZ. We had to let Marie go.

RAY. *Now?* You cut our social worker now?

ROZ. It's horrible. I hate it. I'm asking Ray, what is your backup?

RAY. I thought it was you.

ROZ. I mean on a personal level.

RAY. You have been available on many levels.

ROZ. Yes.

RAY. When did you move to this office?

ROZ. Doctor Lee retired last year.

RAY. So you're running the show.

ROZ. I wouldn't go that far. There wasn't even budget for a new junior hire, so –

RAY. But you got the big office.

ROZ. I got the big office.

RAY. *(Sexual.)* A lot of privacy in this office.

ROZ. That's true.

RAY. Do you ever think about what you and I once did, with some privacy?

ROZ. All the time.

>*(**RAY** touches **ROZ**.)*

RAY. Show me.

ROZ. Ray don't do this.

RAY. Why not?

>*(**RAY** touches **ROZ** intimately. She responds.)*

ROZ. I can't give you what you need. I can't give your sons what they need.

RAY. Let's try.

ROZ. Mikey and Ray Ray will be here.

RAY. I told them to wait in the lobby.

>*(She pulls away.)*

ROZ. You *what*?

RAY. I heard a rumor.

ROZ. So you purposely came to see me alone? To manipulate me, / to –

RAY. Don't make us go where no one knows my kids.

>*(Silence.)*

ROZ. This was an agonizing, soul-searching, very difficult decision made on medical principles alone.

RAY. Their own mother left them. Why wouldn't you?

ROZ. I understand this feels like abandonment. I will talk it through with Mikey and Ray Ray.

RAY. No.

During the transition my family prefers to see Doctor Morada.

ROZ. We have an appointment.

RAY. I will reschedule.

ROZ. I need to say goodbye.

RAY. Nope.

    (**ROZ** *is as generous as possible.*)

ROZ. If you must leave angry, I accept that you leave angry. I cannot afford any principles other than medical, in making decisions now. It's too dire.
University is a research hospital, it's where your sons belong.

RAY. Fuck research. My kids are going to be lab rats.

ROZ. If I'd been in research I might have called this five years ago.

RAY. You did call it.

ROZ. I might have been able to do something. I might have had the confidence, or the clout –

RAY. Poor Doctor Roz without the clout.

ROZ. If I had grown children I would send them to University Hospital.

RAY. But you don't. You have no one.

    (**RAY** *walks out.*)

1991

(Begin overlaps at slashes, not at line breaks.)

RAY.	**ROZ**.
I've gotten very cynical since my boys / were victimized so badly with this whole thing.	I will speak with Ray Leon if he will make an appointment, with counsel.
	But he cannot stand on hospital grounds and / scream.

RAY.	ROZ.
Kagan denies this but the way I see it developing, I can envision the administration and Kagan getting together with the other docs / maybe '82, '83.	
	Nor may he disrupt an event that is a more important part of our budget every / year.
And I could see them doing exactly what the Red Cross did – that's another memo look it up – / and viewing this whole thing in pure economics.	
	This hospital receives less funding every year, as our costs increase. The telethon keeps families together and saves lives.
They held onto my kids while they could still make a buck, then dumped them to / University when they got too expensive. If University was the best place why didn't they go sooner?	I'm being faulted for transferring them to University and I'm being faulted for not transferring them sooner. It's difficult to keep up with the criticism but I'm going to go down swinging.
Maybe there was a trial my son could have gotten, maybe AZT, / if that was the best place why weren't they there in 1985?	They should have been given the best AIDS treatment available at that time?

	Well what was the AIDS treatment? AZT was being worked on, but only with very sick gay men who were basically dying, not hemophiliacs and not / children.
They decided to roll the dice, save a buck, and hope they lucked out.	
But they lost.	AZT is a highly toxic drug. You don't give this for a cold, / okay?
We lost. My sons paid with / their lives.	Eventually it was tested on gay men who were HIV positive but asymptomatic. / *Then* the study came down to hemophiliacs.
We pay, not the hospital and not the doctor.	But in 1987 no one was giving AZT to asymptomatic people. It would have / been crazy.
Practically every hemophiliac in this country born before 1985 is either HIV positive or dead.	
	I too am devastated by the outcome but we must respect established channels.
Ten thousand people.	Children in this building are gravely ill.
THAT'S A GENOCIDE.	

1991

*(Late the same day. **ROZ** enters her bedroom and flicks on the lights, revealing **RAY** in her bed.)*

ROZ. Jesus.

RAY. You snuck out the back.

ROZ. I need you to leave my home.

RAY. Aren't you curious how I got in?

ROZ. I need you to leave.

RAY. I used my key. The one you gave me.

ROZ. That was years ago.

RAY. You didn't change the locks.

ROZ. No, this is my home.

RAY. New master bath.

ROZ. Yes.

RAY. What'd that run you? The tile alone –

ROZ. Get out of here, Ray.

RAY. You wouldn't *meet* with me today. You wouldn't *face* me.

ROZ. It's out of my hands.

RAY. Ray Ray is dead.

ROZ. I learned that. I'm very sorry.

RAY. He got married.

ROZ. I heard.

RAY. High school sweetheart. Who'd think kids in the nineteen-nineties would be so old-fashioned. It was a real pretty wedding. In Presidio Park, looking at the ocean.

ROZ. He loved that park.

RAY. She died first.

ROZ. Jesus.

RAY. Five months pregnant.

*(**ROZ** didn't know about Ray Ray's wife or the pregnancy.)*

ROZ. Can we, continue this conversation over a meal?

RAY. You learn to cook?

ROZ. Let me take you out.

RAY. How many plates of pad thai will it take, Doc Roz?

ROZ. I'm not implying the food (is some kind of payment) –

RAY. You want me gone.

ROZ. I care about you Ray. But we need boundaries.

RAY. You gave me your *key*.

ROZ. That was a mistake.

RAY. Exhibit A.

ROZ. You're going to do what you need to do, Ray.

RAY. What do you think that is?

ROZ. I'm planning to resign, so –

RAY. Early retirement?

ROZ. An academic appointment.

RAY. Good for you.

ROZ. It's a job.

RAY. You were a tourist.

ROZ. Ray I can't even imagine what you're going through.

RAY. No you really can't.

ROZ. On a personal level...

RAY. Finish your sentence.

ROZ. I lost a lot too.

RAY. Oh is that how we're going to play it?

ROZ. Boys I knew twenty years.

RAY. My son is dead. His wife is dead. My grandchild will not be born. Mikey watched the whole thing, knowing he has the same virus. Saw his brother go blind, go crazy, shit himself in a ward with a couple of AIDS skeletons while the skin fell off his face. So Mikey's feeling cheerful.

ROZ. I want to talk about the facts and the feelings.

RAY. Remember the Tylenol scare?

ROZ. Of course –

RAY. Someone died after taking a Tylenol and it was a national alert – boom – Tylenol off the shelves overnight. Remember the Pinto started catching fire?

ROZ. Sure.

RAY. They pulled the cars and *then* they found the flaw.
But you kept selling us your Factor.
That's a crime.

ROZ. Let's take a walk.

RAY. Sorry.

>   (**RAY** *reveals he is handcuffed to Roz's bed, both hands.*)

You got me trapped. Right where you want me.

ROZ. Okay that – this is not how we talk.

RAY. You wouldn't meet.

ROZ. Ray it turned into a mess. I started getting advice –

RAY. Called in the lawyers. Kagan, Rothstein, and Jewstein.

>   (**ROZ** *doesn't take the bait.*)

ROZ. I am so sorry for your loss.

RAY. I bet you are.

ROZ. I wanted to be there for Ray Ray. I didn't know he had been hospitalized.

RAY. Were you waiting on an invitation?

ROZ. I was not waiting on an invitation.

RAY. You wanted to speak at the funeral?

ROZ. No.

RAY. About bad things happening?

ROZ. I met you at the hospital, I *redirected the ambulance* for crying out loud.
I found you in the middle of the night.

RAY. Yes you did.

ROZ. I met you with a dozen vials of Factor. Two coolers.
Was one of those vials the contaminate? Maybe.
But I would do it again.
I would have to.

Ray Ray had a brain hemorrhage.

He was dying that night.

What could I give him except what I had?

RAY. You knew.

ROZ. Ray that's not true.

RAY. You knew the risk. You said so. In 1982 you said it mirrored Hep B, you said AIDS could act like Hep B.

ROZ. We didn't even have a name. I did not say AIDS.

RAY. You made me use a condom in 1982 and you didn't warn the boys until 1984.

ROZ. What can I do for you, Ray?

RAY. Pay up.

ROZ. There's a class action lawsuit / you can –

RAY. You. Pay.

ROZ. No wrongdoing.

RAY. Pay my tuition.

ROZ. You're in school?

RAY. Planning on it.

ROZ. Ray that's fantastic. What subject?

RAY. Biology.

ROZ. Wonderful.

RAY. I have the time.

(Beat.)

ROZ. But to make use of that. Good for you.

RAY. You have condescended to my sons and me from the day we met. Arrogant fucking doctors.

ROZ. I'll pay your tuition.

RAY. Can you afford it?

ROZ. Where will you study?

RAY. Mesa.

ROZ. Yes.

RAY. Then that's not what I want.

ROZ. I figured.

RAY. The first hemophiliac AIDS case was 1981. Why did you keep giving them Factor until 1985?

ROZ. It's a valid question.

RAY. I know it's a valid fucking question.

ROZ. You have to respect time and place and process.

RAY. I don't have to respect fuck all anymore.

ROZ. *(The handcuffs.)* Tell me there's a key to that thing.

RAY. I'm acting up.
You inspired me Roz.
I'm sitting in.
I'm locked down.

ROZ. You hurt a lot.

RAY. I HURT A LOT.

ROZ. Let's get you help.

RAY. Do not manage me. I will not be managed.

ROZ. Where's the key?

RAY. Up my butt.

>   *(Beat.)*

Get your latex gloves, Roz.

ROZ. I am a doctor and I will do that.

RAY. I'll kick in your head.

ROZ. I did not give your sons AIDS.

RAY. No you taught them to give it to themselves.

ROZ. There are medical mistakes, there are changes in knowledge, there is –

RAY. The babies born now are safe.

ROZ. We think so.

RAY. My kids were in that lucky slice, that lucky few years.

ROZ. You want to kick my head in.

RAY. I want to kill you.

ROZ. Yeah.

RAY. All of you. Cutter, Baxter, Bayer. Motherfuckers.

ROZ. Motherfuckers.

RAY. You. You're the motherfucker.

Collected a paycheck every day of this plague.
Sold poison for profit.

ROZ. That was never my personal profit.

RAY. Hemophilia care stayed open. You got the big office. Now you're off to the University.

ROZ. I've been to a lot of funerals, Ray.

RAY. I've been to two.

> (**ROZ** *leaves.* **RAY** *is stuck.*)

Where are you going?
WHERE ARE YOU GOING?
Raymond you did not think this through.

> (**ROZ** *returns with a medical cooler. It bears a biohazard label, the first time we've seen one.*)

What's this?

ROZ. Baxter finally gave out the contaminated lot numbers. Issued a recall. In *1989*.

RAY. Jesus.

ROZ. I kept these because I learned they were selling the bad batches overseas.

RAY. What the fuck?

ROZ. Yup. Japan, China, Korea.
They're selling it now.

RAY. Motherfuckers.

ROZ. Motherfuckers does not begin to describe it, Ray. Pure evil.

RAY. But I'm sure there is some nice lady over there just doing her best.

ROZ. We don't know.
You came to my home and not the drug company.
You came to my home and not the White House.

RAY. Because you personally are a killer.
You are a killer and I can say that to your face.
Killer! Killer! Killer!

> (**ROZ** *wipes her arm with an alcohol swab.*)

RAY. What are you doing?

ROZ. I'm cleaning my skin with antiseptic.
I'm opening the disposable needle.
I'm drawing the contaminated Factor.
You want to kill me?
Get out of your handcuffs and do it.

RAY. The key is in my pocket.

ROZ. I hoped so.

RAY. It would be physically impossible to put it up my butt. Wearing handcuffs.

ROZ. May I touch you?

RAY. Yeah.

> (**ROZ** *retrieves the key from* **RAY**'s *pants pocket. She unlocks his handcuffs.*)
>
> (**ROZ** *uncaps the syringe and hands it to* **RAY**.)

ROZ. Go ahead. You can't hurt me.

> (**RAY** *holds the syringe.*)

RAY. How could you test them and not tell me? Just tell me it was a bad test. Tell me something.

ROZ. I was wrong.

RAY. Yeah, you were.

ROZ. I have felt utterly helpless with you. I do not like that feeling.

RAY. You promised to tell the truth.

ROZ. What good is the truth if there's nothing you can do?

RAY. How could you send us away?

ROZ. I believed it was his best chance.

RAY. A nurse at University didn't know how to find the vein on a hemophiliac. She stabbed and gouged, and pushed, and pulled. His arm swelled this big with black blood. I complained; the doctor said, "This can happen with hemophiliacs," I said, "Not anymore. This is a new age." Ray Ray died suffering from that arm.

ROZ. There's no excuse.

RAY. Wasn't there a doctor who went back to cryo, early?

ROZ. Yeah. In Philadelphia.

RAY. What happened?

ROZ. His patients have a twenty percent rate of infection. Compared to ninety-five percent.

RAY. But not you.

ROZ. No.

RAY. You reached consensus.

ROZ. Yes.

RAY. Did you ever talk to Lee?

ROZ. I waited too long.

RAY. You played it safe.

ROZ. Yeah I did.

  I thought experts knew better than me.
  That's a safe way to think.
  As if grownups are in charge.
  I did that.
  Go ahead.

    (**ROZ** *extends her arm.*)

  I'm numb.
  I'm done.
  I buried too many.
  I have a professorship yeah but fuck it.
  I'd rather give you the satisfaction.
  I'd rather give you what you want.
  You're right I'm bad with boundaries,
  I'd rather die of exposure,
  Die of whatever,
  Die of thrush, pneumocystis, diarrhea,
  I'd rather die letting you in.
  I'd rather die giving you
  Whatever part of me
  You want.

(**RAY** *considers.*)

RAY. Better put the cap back. It's a hazard.

ROZ. Okay.

RAY. And get that shit out of your house.
Dammit. I don't know who to kill.

(*Quiet.*)

ROZ. How have you been?

RAY. I've been like shit.

ROZ. Me too.

RAY. I told Mikey I see men.

ROZ. That was brave.

RAY. He worried I would get AIDS.
Hilarious.
Why is shit distributed how it is?

ROZ. I have no theory.

RAY. I was waiting for the twins to grow up. I thought, hold out. Don't put them through anything more. Just hold out and then they'll be grown, I'll be forty, I'll have a few years to join the party.

ROZ. It's a bad time to join the party.

RAY. What are you gonna teach?

ROZ. Medical history.

RAY. Like, this?

ROZ. No. Maybe. Maybe eventually, this.

RAY. (*New thought.*) One day this will be history.

ROZ. And we will be the survivors.

RAY. Not because we are good.

ROZ. Nope.

RAY. That shitty book, *Shit Happens to Good People*.

ROZ. I was young when I gave you that book.

RAY. There are no natural disasters.
There's evil. There's ignorance. There's profit.

ROZ. They're working on a cure.

RAY. Sure they are. Drug companies made money on the bad blood, now they make money on the disease, one day they'll peddle the fucking cure. Cash cash cash.

Shit happens but humans decide who takes the hit. What fires get put out right away, what burns for years before anyone lifts a fucking finger. There is nothing random about it. Nothing natural.

ROZ. But in how we respond? In who we become to each other?

RAY. Are you still talking about that fucking book?

ROZ. Maybe.

RAY. Because I didn't fucking read it.

ROZ. I don't blame you.

RAY. You don't blame me. How generous.

ROZ. The syringe is there. The offer stands.

RAY. I'm not going to kill you. Or even myself. Though it's tempting.

ROZ. What will we do, Ray?

RAY. I could die of this.

ROZ. Have you been tested?

RAY. Negative. Again last month.

ROZ. Me too.

RAY. Oh?

ROZ. Health worker. High risk.

RAY. Mikey has no symptoms.

ROZ. *(Means it.)* That's significant.

RAY. We're waiting for the other shoe to drop but.

ROZ. Every year he holds out he could be closer. Research money is in.

RAY. A little late.

ROZ. A lot late.

RAY. You promised us seventy years and we got about twelve.

But those twelve were something.

My kids got started as men.

Ray Ray found love.
Mikey is Mikey.
I study biology.
I have one son.

ROZ. You are a spectacular father. Do you know that?

RAY. I miss him.

ROZ. He was your tough guy.

RAY. Tough at the end.

ROZ. We might have a lot of life left.

RAY. I feel a thousand years old.

ROZ. But you're not.

RAY. I should get out of San Diego.

ROZ. Great.

RAY. The best hospitals are in San Francisco anyway.

ROZ. Huge capacity. Fine doctors.

RAY. So maybe I get there.
And Mikey survives.
And maybe I find a lover.
And maybe you find a lover.

ROZ. And maybe someone will care this happened.
And maybe the ones who don't care now will care then.
And maybe the ones who care now will not care then.
And a cure will come, but not for all.

RAY. And the baths will shut.
And the bars will shut.
And gay couples will buy condos
And we will want fucking condos
And I don't want a condo.
I waited to be free.
I can't recall why.
To protect my kids
from shame?
from harm?
from me?

And maybe I will be free and maybe I won't.

And there will be no reason any of them died.

ROZ. And these deaths were preventable, but death is not preventable.

RAY. And one day I will be old and you will be older – you're older than me right?

ROZ. I'm pretty sure.

RAY. I will be old and you will be older and maybe – can I say this?

ROZ. I will be dying.

RAY. Possibly here.

In the bed.

ROZ. Possibly I was a professor for many years.

RAY. And let's say Mikey makes it.

And let's say times are different.

And I will talk to you on a television phone.

ROZ. And I will catch your eye on the television phone and beckon you.

Ray, come here.

We shared so much.

RAY. And I will show up with my guitar

And the lines my boys cut near my mouth.

Lines I will not fix although we gays can be a little vain.

I will kiss my lover in our condo and I will board a plane to see you.

To sing you out.

Because you deserve it.

ROZ. Because this is a love song.

And if it's not I don't want to hear it.

RAY. And I would not trade one hour with my sons for a year in Hawaii.

Evie was an asshole.

She missed everything.

ROZ. I'll be blind.

RAY. You'll be blind?

ROZ. I will be completely dependent.

I will be led around by others.

I will profess history in my blindness.

RAY. Okay you'll be blind.

And you will be –

ROZ. I will be dying. As we do. In our time.

> (**RAY** *holds* **ROZ**.)
>
> (*He sings the beginning of something like Elvis's "Can't Help Falling in Love." It's slow and sentimental.**)
>
> (**RAY** *sings for* **ROZ**, *then for the boys, then for the world.*)

End of Play

---

*A license to produce *Roz and Ray* does not include a performance license for "Can't Help Falling in Love." The publisher and author suggest that the licensee contact ASCAP or BMI to ascertain the music publisher and contact such music publisher to license or acquire permission for performance of the song. If a license or permission is unattainable for "Can't Help Falling in Love," the licensee may not use the song in *Roz and Ray* but should create an original composition in a similar style or use a similar song in the public domain. For further information, please see Music Use Note on page 3.

www.ingramcontent.com/pod-product-compliance
Lightning Source LLC
LaVergne TN
LVHW020352260326
834688LV00045B/1684